UN LIBRO TIGRILLO

A GROUNDWOOD BOOK

TORONTO • VANCOUVER • BERKELEY

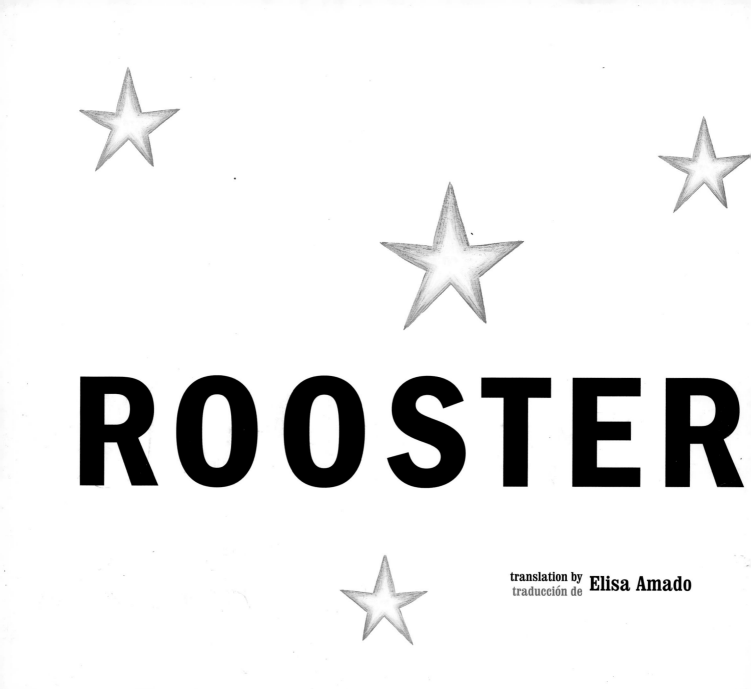

ROOSTER

translation by
traducción de **Elisa Amado**

GALLO

by / por **Jorge Luján**

pictures by / ilustrado por **Manuel Monroy**

For John Oliver Simon and Rebecca Parfitt with much love —JL
To Fernanda, Emilio, Sebastián and Jorgito with all my love —MM

Para John Oliver Simon y Rebecca Parfitt con mucho cariño —JL
Con todo mi amor para Fernanda, Emilio, Sebastián y Jorgito —MM

Text copyright © 2004 by Jorge Luján
Illustration copyright © 2004 by Manuel Monroy
Translation copyright © 2004 by Elisa Amado
Second printing 2004

Groundwood Books / Douglas & McIntyre
720 Bathurst Street, Suite 500, Toronto, Ontario M5S 2R4
Distributed in the USA by Publishers Group West
1700 Fourth Street, Berkeley, CA 94710

We acknowledge for their financial support of our publishing program the Canada Council for the Arts, the Government of Canada through the Book Publishing Industry Development Program (BPIDP), the Ontario Arts Council and the Government of Ontario through the Ontario Media Development Corporation's Ontario Book Initiative.

ONTARIO ARTS COUNCIL
CONSEIL DES ARTS DE L'ONTARIO

National Library of Canada Cataloging in Publication
Luján, Jorge
Rooster / by Jorge Luján; pictures by Manuel Monroy = Gallo / por Jorge Luján ; ilustrado por Manuel Monroy.
Text in English and Spanish.
ISBN 0-88899-558-X
I. Monroy, Manuel II. Title. III. Title: Gallo.
PZ73.E44Ro 2004   j861   C2003-903467-4

Printed and bound in China

Texto © 2004 de Jorge Luján
Ilustración © 2004 de Manuel Monroy
Segunda impresión 2004

Groundwood Books / Douglas & McIntyre
720 Bathurst Street, Suite 500, Toronto, Ontario M5S 2R4
Distribuido en los Estados Unidos por Publishers Group West
1700 Fourth Street, Berkeley, CA 94710

Agradecemos el apoyo financiero otorgado a nuestro programa de publicaciones por el Canada Council for the Arts, el Gobierno de Canada por medio del Book Publishing Industry Development Program (BPIDP), el Ontario Arts Council y el Gobierno de Ontario por medio del Ontario Media Development Corporation's Ontario Book Initiative.

National Library of Canada Cataloging in Publication
Luján, Jorge
Rooster / by Jorge Luján; pictures by Manuel Monroy = Gallo / por Jorge Luján ; ilustrado por Manuel Monroy.
Text in English and Spanish. ISBN 0-88899-558-X
I. Monroy, Manuel II. Title. III. Title: Gallo.
PZ73.E44Ro 2004   j861   C2003-903467-4

Impreso y encuadernado en China

El gallo abre su pico

The rooster opens its beak

y sale el sol.

and up comes the sun.

El sol abre su mano
The sun opens its hand

y nace el día.

and the day is born.

El día se asombra
cuando la noche

The day is surprised when night

tiende su capa
y la colma de estrellas

spreads its cloak and fills it with stars

para que coma el gallo

that the rooster can eat

y vuelva transparente

and so clear the sky

al nuevo día.

for a new day.

El gallo abre su pico
y sale el sol.
El sol abre su mano
y nace el día.
El día se asombra cuando la noche
tiende su capa y la colma de estrellas
para que coma el gallo
y vuelva transparente
al nuevo día.

The rooster opens its beak
and up comes the sun.
The sun opens its hand
and the day is born.
The day is surprised when night
spreads its cloak and fills it with stars
that the rooster can eat
and so clear the sky for
a new day.